THE FIVE

ROLLATINIS

STORY AND PICTURES BY JAN B. BALET

AMMO

The Five Rollatinis
by Jan B. Balet

First Published, 1959

First AMMO Books Edition, 2015

Special thanks to the Balet family.

Acquisitions Editor: Gloria Fowler
Production: Megan Shoemaker
Copy Edit: Sara Richmond

ISBN: 9781623260538

Library of Congress Control Number: 2015943779

To enjoy the wonderful world of AMMO Books, please visit us at ammobooks.com.

AND ONE FINE DAY the circus came to town. The windows of the butcher shop were sparkling with fierce lion posters. The grocer had astounding pictures of extraordinary, daring, death-defying high-wire acts. But the best of all this display was to be seen at the bakery. There over the counter hung a glorious picture of the peerless prodigies of equestrian phenomena, The Five Magnificent Rollatinis and Their Big Wonder Horse Ammonia. Every night when they performed to thundering applause, Bambino stood with tears in his eyes, watching his family and wishing they would let him be part of the great act. He just knew that the five Rollatinis were the greatest bareback riders on this earth. It said so on the advertisement. He was convinced he had talent, too,

1 CIRCUS

and besides, he wanted to be with his family. He loved them. And they loved him, too. It was not very hard to explain, but for him very difficult to understand, that there was only so much space on a horse and that this space was taken up by the five great magnificent Rollatinis. Bambino pleaded with his father. He begged him to think of something. So Pappa very patiently started all over again. A horse is only so tall, so-o-o wide, so-o-o-o long, and there was hardly space enough on good old Ammonia for the five of them. It was really nobody's fault. The five Rollatinis were all over the billboards before Bambino was born. His father promised to think up a solution. As long as Bambino wanted to be with the circus, Pappa

suggested that there might be an opportunity with the lions. He also silently hoped that Bambino might forget all about it. Oh, but not his boy! He knew what he wanted. Bambino knew the lions very well and they had known him since he was a baby. The big old grandfather lion was supposed to be verrrry fierrrrrrce, but Bambino knew that this was only on account of a frequent toothache. After he slipped him an aspirin, he purred just like a kitten. There were really no problems about this job. Bambino just stood around, made jokes with the grandfather lion about the so verrry, verrrry fierrrce-looking lion tamer. That night, after the performance, he asked his father if he had thought of something, because he wanted

1 TIGER 3 LIONS

to be one of them. Pappa agreed that it was not much fun to work for the old lion tamer and maybe he might like it more with the elephants. Pappa had a talk with the General who took care of the gray, mighty giants. Bambino was well acquainted with all of the towering monsters and they knew him. But somehow he really liked the perfume of horses much better than the smell of elephants. That smell had nothing to do with home and he wanted so much to be with his family. "Maybe the trouble is with the animals," Pappa Rollatini thought. "Maybe the clowns will do the trick." They were the ones that used to babysit with Bambino. They were the ones who used to dry his tears when

6 CLOWNS

he fell and make him laugh again. For awhile it was fun, but even the laughmakers with all their riotous color and their wonderful tricks could not get his one-track mind off the idea of being with his family, the great riding Rollatinis. He told his father and his mother that he liked the fierce lions, that he admired the daring lion tamer, that he enjoyed the super-duper tons of the elephants and their famous general, that he adored the colorful clowns, but that he loved his own family and wanted to be with them. They all agreed that this was a real problem, but the fact was that the horse's back was only so big and that this space was taken up. Now Mister Rollatini had a friend whose name was Sasha. That was short for Alexander, but everybody called him Sam. Sasha, I mean Sam, owned the bears.

4 BEARS

Pappa asked Sam what he could suggest to do about Bambino's problem. Well, Sam thought, maybe the boy needs a challenge. "Now I have a bear that dances, but it cannot ride on a bicycle. I know that Bambino and the beast are on speaking terms. Maybe he will ride a bicycle for him. For me he will only dance." It was quite a chore and it took quite some time to teach him. That animal sure was a big bag of fur.

But finally came the big evening. The bear rode the bicycle all around the ring and waved his paw. It was a stupendous success. Mister Rollatini came to congratulate his little son. Bambino, all worn out, said it was really not such a big thing. "All you need is a bear and a bicycle.

Now, when it comes to riding on Ammonia—that would really be an achievement." Pappa sure was tired of hearing the same old thing. He took his son by the hand and said to him earnestly, "Please make one more try with the acrobats, and if you do not like that either— well we will just have to do something. After all Bambino is one of the Rollatinis and, and—" "I know," answered Bambino, "but I get so lonely and homesick when I am not with all of you. But, OK, I promise I will try." For a moment it was wonderful, high up under the roof of the tent. The lights, the glitter, the flashing sparkle, the breathless upturned faces of the audience almost made Bambino forget his troubles.

9 ACROBATS

But when he looked down, he could just get a glimpse of the five great Rollatinis getting ready for their act. Then he knew only too well that there never would be nor ever could be a substitute for being a member of the family.

After that he told his parents that he would never be happy with strangers. They knew all along what he meant. They all started talking at once, just like any other family. All of a sudden, Pappa got up and announced very quietly, "I think I have found a solution." "What is it?" "What kind of an idea did you get?" "Tell us!" "Please let us know!!" But Mister Rollatini said very grandly, "It is going to be a surprise!" And a permanent surprise it was, because the poster in the bakery had a beautiful, red sticker added to it that announced ....

THE
PEERLESS PRODIGIES
OF
EQUESTRIAN PHENOMENA

THE

~~FIVE~~ SIX

ROLLATINIS

AND THEIR WONDER HORSES

AMMONIA

&

AMMONITA